Nancy Alberts

Interior and cover illustrations
by Fredericka Ribes

A
LITTLE APPLE
PAPERBACK

SCHOLASTIC INC.
New York Toronto London Auckland Sydney

ISBN 0-590-25234-8

12 11   2/0

Printed in the U.S.A.   40

First Scholastic printing, April 1996

To DeWitt and Mary Markham, my parents,
who always made me feel like a star.

1

Beep, beep.

Kelly McKay reached under her pillow and turned off her alarm clock.

Trish, her little sister, was still asleep in the bed next to hers. Good. The pillow had muffled the sound.

Today Kelly wanted extra time by herself to get ready for school.

She looked at her calendar. It was the first Wednesday in May. A gold star was on the date.

Today Mrs. Glocken, the music teacher, would pick some second graders to have special parts for the Spring Concert. Kelly wanted to be picked. For once in her life, she wanted to be more than plain old ordinary Kelly. She wanted to be a star.

Kelly got dressed and tiptoed down the stairs. Dad was feeding her little brother, Scooter, in the kitchen.

"K-K, K-K!" Scooter called from his high chair. He gave a wide, double-toothed smile. Mushy brown oatmeal dribbled down his chin.

Kelly took a napkin and wiped his face. "Hi Scooter, you messy monkey," she said. "Hi Dad."

"Good morning," said Dad. "You're an early bird."

Kelly twirled around. "I think it's my lucky day."

"It is? Why?"

Kelly told him about the concert.

Dad gave Scooter his bottle. "I hope your teacher chooses you," he said. "But don't set your heart on it. What if she doesn't?"

Kelly shrugged. "Then I don't get picked. No big deal."

But she knew her words were fake as soon as they left her lips. Her heart was set on having a special part in the concert. And it would be a big, bad deal if she didn't get picked.

Mrs. Glocken just had to pick her. Her voice wasn't loud, but she could sing the right notes and all the right words for the songs.

She headed down to the basement bathroom. No one could hear her or bother her there.

Kelly looked in the mirror as she combed her hair. She wished she weren't so plain-looking. Then Mrs. Glocken would be sure not to forget about her.

The only thing people noticed was her hair. But it was dark red and straight, not curly and bright like her two brothers and two sisters.

She was short, too. Her sister Trish was almost as tall, even though she was just in kindergarten. Mom and Dad always said Kelly was as small as a bird.

Maybe that wasn't so bad. The longest song in the concert was all about a bird.

"It's showtime!" Kelly said to the mirror. She turned on the hot water in the shower stall. Then she stood on the toilet seat to see in the mirror better.

She sang the concert songs as loud as she could. Steam from the water lifted her voice and filled the bathroom. Her voice sounded big. No wonder Mom sang in the shower.

At the end of the last song, she stretched her arms high like a rock singer and bowed. She looked in the mirror, fogged with steam, and saw a flash of bright copper curls. Trish!

Kelly turned around so fast her stocking feet slid off the toilet seat. Her backside landed on the lid with a thud.

"Oo! Ouch! Trish!" she hiccuped. "How long have you been in here? Why didn't you knock? Why aren't you in bed?"

Trish had a question of her own. "What are you doing?"

"Nothing!" said Kelly. "You're supposed to be asleep."

"How could I sleep? You woke everyone."

"How could I wake everyone from down here?"

Trish shook her head. "I don't know. All I know is you were loud. Come on. Mom wants you to have breakfast."

Kelly followed Trish up the stairs, light-footed. Loud. Trish said she was loud. Maybe Mrs. Glocken would think she was loud, too.

2

Loud was the word for the kitchen. The rest of the McKays filled the room with noise.

"Here comes the Fanny of the Opera," said Joe, clapping.

Julie, his twin, laughed. "Tell me, Fanny, when is your next early morning concert? Let me know so I can stuff cotton in my ears."

"Hush, you two," said Mom. "Your singing sounded pretty," she told Kelly. "But next time, wait until everyone's up. Your voice carried right up through the vents to the second floor. You also wasted a lot of hot water."

"I'm sorry," said Kelly. Mainly she was sorry to hear about the vents. So that was why everyone had heard her. Not because her voice was loud.

Trish was giggling. "Fanny! Fanny of the Opera! That's funny, Joe."

Dad washed out his coffee mug. "Kelly's hoping to get picked for a special singing part today," he said. "She needs our good wishes, not our jokes."

"Heck, I was just kidding," said Joe.

"Sure," said Julie. "You'll be the star of the show, Kelly."

Trish tapped on Kelly's arm. "Will you really be a star?"

"I hope so," Kelly whispered.

Mom hugged her. "You're already a star, honey. You'll always be a star in my heart."

Mom's hug felt good. Her words made Kelly feel like she could do anything.

After breakfast, the twins left for middle school. Kelly walked with Trish to the bus stop. The Spring Concert songs jangled in her head. Her steps kept the beat on the sidewalk.

Trish sat with a friend on the bus. Kelly was glad. She needed some time alone to let Mom's words sink deeper. *You're already a star.*

The bus took off. It stopped twice. At the third stop, a big bunch of kids got on. The last one on was Liza Wilson, Kelly's best friend.

She came slowly up the aisle. Her arms were straight out in front of her. Her eyes were half-closed, like a sleepwalker's. She flopped down and put her head on Kelly's lap.

Kelly giggled. "Liza, what are you doing?"

Liza's eyes were closed. She started to snore.

"Wake up, Liza," said Kelly. "Time for school."

Liza rubbed her eyes. "Huh? Oh hi, Kelly. Good morning."

"You're silly," said Kelly.

"Silly and tired," said Liza. "Dead tired."

"How come?"

Liza yawned. "I couldn't sleep a wink last night."

"What's the matter?"

"I was worried I won't have a special part in the Spring Concert."

"Really? Me, too."

"Aw. You'll get picked. No problem. You have a good voice."

"Thanks." Kelly smiled at Liza. What a nice thing for her to say.

But suddenly, she felt more worried. It sounded like Liza wanted a part as much as she did. How many others in her second-grade class felt the same way? How many would be trying just as hard to be a star?

3

In school, Kelly could think of nothing but music class. She kept listening for a rolling rumble out in the hall of Featherstone School. Finally she heard it. Mrs. Glocken was pushing her piano on wheels.

It was almost ten o'clock. Time for music.

Kelly sat up straight. She wanted to look ready.

Mrs. Hall cleared a spot for the piano and opened the door.

The piano came wheeling in, followed by a huffing Mrs. Glocken. Mrs. Hall helped her lift the upside-down piano bench off the top of the piano. "Sing like canaries, class," she joked as she left the room.

"Happy, happy morning, boys and girls," sang Mrs. Glocken. Mrs. Glocken sang almost everything she said.

She sat down on the bench with a bounce. Her blond curls bobbed against her ears. She played some lively notes with her big white hands. Her red fingernails clicked on the keys.

"Sing, sing a song. Sing out loud. Sing out long," the class sang. It was what they always sang first. Everyone knew the words by heart.

"Wonderful!" sang Mrs. Glocken. "Our Spring Concert is next Friday. Only ten days away. As you know, it will be a concert just for kindergarten, first, and second graders. But only second graders will have special parts."

There was a rustle of excitement in the room. Liza smiled at Kelly. Her fingers were crossed. Kelly crossed hers, too.

"Since there are two second-grade classes," said Mrs. Glocken, "I will pick a few children from each room."

She turned around and plugged in the record player.

Broderick blew a big pink gum bubble while

Mrs. Glocken's back was turned. Liza reached out to pop it.

Some of the kids snickered. Liza made a funny face at Kelly. Kelly acted like she didn't see her. She didn't want anything to spoil her chances for a special part.

Mrs. Glocken put on the concert record.

"A Frog Went A-Courtin' " was the first concert song. Mrs. Glocken looked around the room as the class sang. Kelly hoped she noticed how well she was singing.

"Wonderful," sang Mrs. Glocken, clapping. "Stand up, Timmy."

Timmy stood up. He looked like he was going to cry.

"Isn't that cute?" said Mrs. Glocken.

Timmy was wearing a bright green sweatsuit with Kermit the Frog on the front.

"Will you be the frog in the concert?" asked Mrs. Glocken. "You can wear that outfit. It'll be perfect!"

Timmy's ears turned red. He didn't say anything.

Kelly raised her hand. She could be the frog if Timmy didn't want to. She had a green jumpsuit.

And she could *ribbit* like a frog. Trish and Scooter loved it. Maybe Mrs. Glocken would

13

love it, too, and pick her to be the frog.

"Timmy won't do it," Broderick called out. "He's too scared. I'll be the frog. Watch me hop."

He got on the floor and hopped down the aisle. The children giggled. Other kids tried hopping.

Kelly sat still with her hand as high as a flag. Mrs. Glocken wouldn't pick anyone who was being rowdy.

"Back in your seats!" sang Mrs. Glocken in a loud one-tone staccato. She looked at Timmy. "You'll do it, Timmy, won't you?"

Timmy nodded.

Kelly dropped her hand on her desk. She couldn't believe it. The shyest boy in second grade was going to be a star just because he wore a Kermit the Frog sweatsuit.

4

Mrs. Glocken turned on the record player again. There were two more songs for Mrs. Hall's room. Kelly still had a chance for a special part.

"A Bicycle Built for Two" was the next song. Kelly loved the swinging, snappy tune.

"Daisy, Daisy, give me your answer, do." She smiled at Mrs. Glocken as she sang. She wanted to shout, "Pick me, pick me. I can be Daisy!"

When the song was over, Mrs. Glocken said, "I'm going to ask some fifth graders to draw a two-seater bike on poster board. I'll need a boy and a girl to pretend they are riding as they sing."

Almost all the girls raised their hands. Some

made "oo-ooh" sounds like they were in pain. Bree waved both hands in the air. Kelly raised her hand quietly and high. Mrs. Glocken never called on moaners.

But then Anna Mae called out, "We have a real two-seater bike. It's called a tandem. I know my mom will let me bring it in for the concert."

"Really?" said Mrs. Glocken. She pressed her palms together. "That's perfect, Anna Mae. Then you can be Daisy."

Kelly felt crushed. Mrs. Glocken was so unfair. Wearing a green sweatsuit or having a tandem had nothing to do with singing.

"Let's see," said Mrs. Glocken. "Let's have Mike be Daisy's boyfriend."

The boys went "Woo-oo!" The girls giggled. Anna Mae blushed and hugged herself as if Mike had asked her to marry him.

Kelly looked at Mike. He didn't look very pleased. But he didn't say no.

There was one more song. It was a long song about a baby robin, learning to fly. Kelly crossed her fingers again.

Mrs. Glocken watched everyone as they sang. Most of the kids didn't know the words very well. They just moved their mouths with the music.

Kelly knew the words perfectly. She sang as

loud as she could except for the whistling part. Kelly couldn't whistle.

Mrs. Glocken took off the record. "Some of you aren't singing or whistling. Let's try it again without the record player."

Oh, no, thought Kelly.

At the whistling part, she puckered her lips and blew, but all that came out was air.

Broderick's chewing gum shot out of his mouth like a spitball. The gum hit the piano and landed on the bench.

Kelly put her hand over her mouth and tried not to laugh. Others couldn't hold back their giggles.

Mrs. Glocken didn't notice. Neither did Liza. Liza whistled like she had been hatched in a nest.

"Wonderful, Liza!" sang Mrs. Glocken. "You'll make a perfect baby robin for our concert."

Liza turned and gave a thumbs-up sign to Kelly. Kelly tried to smile, but her mouth froze. She should feel glad for Liza. But she didn't.

She put her head down on her desk and kept it there while the class practiced the three songs for the other second-grade class.

"Who can fold paper neatly?" asked Mrs. Glocken.

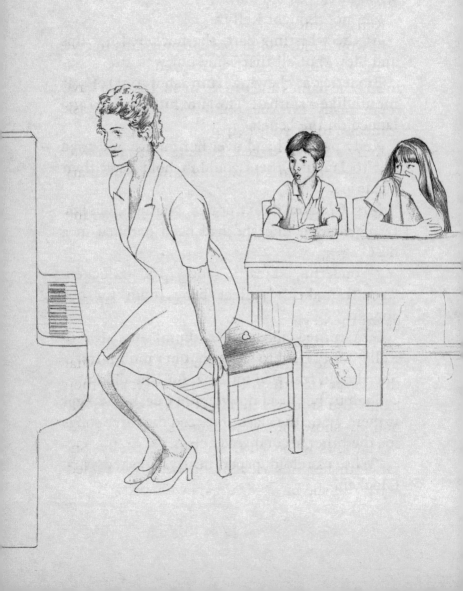

Kelly's head popped up. She put up her hand. There was still hope. Maybe there was a part with a folded paper hat.

"I think Kelly must be good at folding neatly," sang Mrs. Glocken.

Kelly beamed.

"I would like you to fold the programs to give to the parents," said Mrs. Glocken. "I just have to add the names and run them off. I should have them ready for you tomorrow. You can ask someone to be your helper."

Kelly's smile sagged. Folding programs was not a special part. It was a plain old ordinary stupid job.

Mrs. Glocken had tricked her. Kelly couldn't wait for music class to end.

Mrs. Glocken sat down at the piano and played the song they always sang at the end of music class. Her clickety fingers flew up and down the keyboard.

"If you're happy and you know it, clap your hands." The children sang loudly. They did what the words told them to do. They clapped their hands and stomped their feet. They yelled "Ya-hoo" to show they were happy.

The kids whooped it up. But not Kelly. She sat with her lips zipped and her arms folded. What did she have to be happy about?

Mrs. Glocken got up and set the bench upside down on the piano top. As she wheeled the piano toward the door, the children giggled into their hands.

Broderick's gum was stuck on the back of Mrs. Glocken's black dress like a big pink polka dot. Kelly was glad. Mrs. Glocken deserved it.

5

Kelly walked head down into the girls' room at bathroom break. She pushed open a stall door.

"Get out!" squealed someone. "I'm in here." It sounded like Anna Mae.

"Oops," said Kelly. "Sorry." She pulled the door shut.

"Is that you, Kelly?" Anna Mae asked from behind the door.

"Yes."

"The lock's broken on the door. Will you please hold the door shut until I'm done?"

"Okay," said Kelly. But she didn't really want to.

Anna Mae sang loudly off-key, "You'll look

sweet upon the seat of a bicycle built for two."

What a show-off!

In the next stall, she heard whistling. It had to be Liza.

After a flush, Liza came out with a smile a mile wide. "Hey, Kelly, old pal, isn't it exciting? I can't believe Mrs. Glocken picked me to be the baby robin. And you're in charge of the programs! I'll be your helper."

Without waiting for an answer, Liza skipped over to the sink. She whistled as she soaped her hands.

Kelly felt a knot in her stomach. Liza wasn't the show-off type, but now she sounded as braggy as Anna Mae.

Bree came into the bathroom. "Oh, Kelly, I'll fold the programs with you, okay?"

Kelly didn't know Bree very well, but she was nice. Maybe she also felt bad about not being picked for a special part.

"Okay, Bree," said Kelly.

"Thanks a bunch!" said Bree.

Liza spun around and looked at Kelly. "Wait a minute. I asked you first." She sounded hurt.

"I know," said Kelly. "But you already have a part."

Bree tugged on Kelly's arm. "There's only a half day of school tomorrow. May I come over to your house after school? We can fold the programs then."

"Sure. I guess so."

"Kelly McKay!" said Liza. "You and I always get together on half days. I was going to ask you to come over to my house tomorrow."

Kelly loved going to Liza's house. But today she didn't even feel like talking to her.

"Sorry, Liza. We have to get the programs done."

Liza folded her arms. "No fair. What's wrong with you today?"

The knot in Kelly's stomach felt tighter. "Nothing," she said. She knocked on the stall door. "Come on, Anna Mae, hurry up." There was a flush.

"I'm coming," Anna Mae said in a sing-song Mrs. Glocken voice.

"Liza," said Anna Mae, as she came out. "You can come to my house tomorrow. We can practice our parts. I'll even let you ride the tandem."

"Really?" said Liza. "Great!"

Kelly stomped into the stall. She felt mad at the world. "Hey, Anna Mae, hold the door."

"I can't, Kelly. I have to comb my hair. It's a mess."

Kelly gritted her teeth.

"I'll hold it," said Bree.

"Thanks," Kelly mumbled. Then she heard Anna Mae whisper, "I know what's wrong with Kelly McKay. She's just jealous."

Kelly felt her face burning. How dare Anna Mae say such a thing to her very own best friend. But Kelly wasn't acting like a best friend. She was treating Liza rotten. She hadn't even said, "Congratulations."

Anna Mae was right. She was plain old ordinary jealous.

6

"Here's a seat," Kelly called out as Liza got on the bus the next morning. Liza looked around as if she didn't know where to sit. Finally she sat next to Kelly with a loud sigh.

Kelly swallowed hard. "Liza, I'm sorry about yesterday. I wanted Mrs. Glocken to pick me so much. I felt really bad. I still do."

She bit her lip. Then she took a deep breath. "But I'm glad for you."

Liza smiled at Kelly. "Thanks. Forget about yesterday."

Kelly smiled back. "Bree's riding the bus home with me today. I wish you were coming, too. You can if you want."

"I can't. I'm riding Anna Mae's bus to her house."

"Really? I didn't think you even liked her."

"She's all right," said Liza. "Her brother's going to let us take turns riding on the back of the tandem."

Kelly pictured Liza laughing and whistling as she rode around on Anna Mae's two-seater bike.

"It's supposed to rain," said Kelly. A blanket of gray clouds covered the sky. She couldn't help wishing it would rain all afternoon.

Kelly got what she wished for and more. By the time the half day was over, it was raining buckets.

Right before the bell rang, Mrs. Glocken burst into the classroom. "Excuse me, Mrs. Hall. This is for Kelly."

She handed Kelly a white plastic bag with a stack of pale blue papers inside.

"Here are the programs, dear. Fold them in thirds, like the sample inside, okee-dokie?"

Kelly nodded.

"Have a happy day," Mrs. Glocken sang as she left.

Anna Mae crooned, "Ooooh! Let me see the programs."

"Not now," said Kelly. She closed the end of the bag. She never wanted to see them. Not if they didn't have her name on them.

Outside, Kelly slipped the plastic bag under her bright pink poncho. No matter how she felt about the programs, she had to keep them dry.

Inside the bus, Bree brushed water off her backpack. "I should have brought my umbrella."

"You can share my poncho," said Kelly. "It's gigantic. It used to be my sister's."

"Thanks. You're lucky to have a big sister."

"I also have two brothers and a little sister, Trish," said Kelly. "She'll be getting on the bus soon."

"Wow!" said Bree. "It's just me and Mom at my house. My dad lives in Florida. They're divorced."

"That's too bad," said Kelly.

Trish ran up the aisle, dripping wet. She squeezed in next to Kelly.

"Can't you sit somewhere else?" Kelly asked. "And where's your raincoat?"

"I don't know. I looked in the lost and found."

Kelly shook her head. Now she'd have to keep three people dry under her poncho.

"Hi. I'm Bree. I'm coming over to your house today."

"Bree. That's a funny name," said Trish. "Sounds like the fancy cheese Mom has at parties."

Kelly elbowed Trish. "Shh. Don't be rude."

Bree laughed. "Brie cheese is spelled B-R-I-E. I spell my name like this."

She leaned across Kelly to show Trish her necklace. The necklace had four square yellow beads with a letter on each.

"B-R-E-E," spelled Trish. "Those beads look like cheese cubes. Yum!" She pretended to pull the beads off and eat them. The two girls got into a laughing fit.

"Hey, you two," said Kelly. "Stop crowding me. I feel like a sandwich."

That made Bree and Trish laugh more. "She's a Brie cheese sandwich," said Trish.

"No," said Bree. "A Kelly sandwich. A peanut-butter-and-Kelly sandwich! Get it, Kelly?"

Sure she got it, but she didn't think it was very funny. Bree seemed to like Trish better than her.

Then she had a worse thought. What if Liza and Anna Mae were having this much fun right now as they rode a different bus to Anna Mae's house?

Kelly didn't like feeling so jealous. When she got off the bus, she decided to leave her grumpy mood behind.

She spread the poncho wide. Bree and Trish

scooted under. They put their heads in the armholes.

"Now I feel like a three-headed, six-legged flamingo," said Kelly. Bree and Trish giggled again. Bree had a high, tickly laugh. Kelly got the giggles, too.

Bree and Trish flapped each side of the poncho like wings.

"We're flying!" squealed Trish.

They came to a big puddle. Trish went one way. Bree went the other way. Kelly stumbled. The bag of programs slipped from under her arm and plopped into the puddle.

Kelly screamed. Quickly she fished out the bag. But it was too late. Water had seeped in. The programs were dark blue on the edges.

Kelly wasn't laughing anymore.

7

"Come on in, duckies," said Mom. She held the kitchen screen door open.

Kelly wanted to rush into Mom's arms, but she let Trish and Bree go first.

"Hello, Bree. It's so nice to have you."

"Hi, Mrs. McKay."

"We aren't duckies, Mommy," said Trish. "We were a three-headed, six-legged flamingo."

"Oh my," said Mom. "Let me help you, Kelly." She took off the wet poncho and hung it on a hook. "What's wrong, honey?"

Kelly held the plastic bag with clenched fingers. She was afraid if she talked, she would cry.

"She dropped the programs in a puddle," said Bree. "They got all wet."

Kelly's eyes filled with tears. It sounded like Bree was blaming her.

"I didn't mean to."

"Of course not," said Mom. "Let me see."

Kelly opened the bag and took out the pile of programs. Already the edges were curled into waves of blue.

Mom took the programs. "Don't worry, honey. They'll be all right." She put them on the counter and set three big cookbooks on top. "There. Just let them be until they dry."

Kelly felt like a beam of sunlight had burst through the clouds and lit up the kitchen. The programs would be all right.

While Trish showed Mom her school papers, Kelly pulled Bree into the hall. "Come on. I'll show you my room."

They started up the stairs. Bree stopped. "Wait," she said. "What a nice picture!" She was looking at a family photo in a gold frame.

Kelly liked the photo. It was a good picture of everyone. "This is Scooter," she said, pointing. "He's taking a nap now."

"Aww! He's adorable," said Bree.

"These are the twins," said Kelly. "Joe is a

computer whiz and Julie is the only girl on the boys' baseball team. She's a star pitcher."

"Wow!" said Bree. "That's so neat!"

Kelly pointed to Trish. "Of course you know her already. Did you know she models clothes for stores? Her pictures are in catalogs."

"Golly galoshes!" said Bree. "Your family sounds famous!"

Kelly smiled. She had never thought of her family as famous before. But maybe they were in a way.

Then Bree turned to Kelly. "What about you?"

"That's me, silly," said Kelly, pointing to the photo.

Then she realized that Bree wanted to know what was special about Kelly.

Kelly stood as mute as a moose head, staring at the photo. Trish, Julie, and Joe. They all did something special that made them stand out. Even Scooter. He was so cute, he might as well have a star right on his forehead.

But Kelly was just plain old Kelly.

8

It was way past Kelly's bedtime Thursday night. Trish was in bed, sound asleep. Kelly was in bed, but she was far from falling asleep.

It was quiet enough to sleep. Dark enough, too. Just a dim light from the street lamp and a skinny moon shone through the window. All that glowed inside were the night-light and the hands on Kelly's clock.

She tried to count the white pom-poms on the curtains, pretending they were sheep. But she kept losing track.

She got out her diary, a pencil, and a flashlight. She shined the light on a clean page and wrote in small, neat letters.

Dear Diary, Bree was here today. She's so nice and funny, too.

Kelly tapped the pencil on her chin, thinking. She liked Bree. Bree had made a fuss over her neat room and all of her special things.

But she had made a bigger fuss over everyone else. She had counted Julie's trophies twice. She had oohed and aahed over Trish's modeling scrapbook. She had played with Scooter and fed him his lunch. Then Joe had let Bree use the computer almost all afternoon.

When it got sunny, Kelly and Bree had gone outside.

We had fun on the swing set, she wrote.

Kelly smiled, remembering. They had acted like monkeys. But then Bree had joined the twins in a Wiffle ball game.

Kelly wrote a long sentence in her diary. *I like Bree, but she likes my family better than me.*

Kelly didn't really blame Bree. Everyone else was much more exciting than she was. If only she was special at something.

She used to think she was a good singer. But Mrs. Glocken hadn't picked her to be a star.

All I am is neat, she wrote.

But she wasn't even good at being neat any-more. She had messed up the programs. They still weren't dry. So she and Bree didn't get to fold them after all.

Kelly frowned. She held the pencil tightly and wrote in big, sloppy letters. *I'm not neat anymore. That's OK. I'm sick of being neat. But now I'm nothing.*

Kelly signed her name with a scribble that filled up the rest of the page. She felt worse than before. But at least she was tired. She put everything back in place. Then she shut her eyes to keep the tears in.

A bad dream woke her. When Kelly opened her eyes, her room was pitch-black. The moon had moved and the street lamp was off. So was the night-light. All she could see were the hands on her clock. Two-thirty.

She clicked on the lamp on her bedside table. It didn't come on. She got her flashlight and went out into the hall. She tried the hall light. That didn't work either. She made her way to Mom and Dad's room.

Dad snored softly.

Kelly sat on Mom's side of the bed and stared at her.

Mom stirred. "What is it?" she mumbled.

"All the lights are out," whispered Kelly.

Mom was awake now. She sat up and looked out the window. "The whole neighborhood's dark," she whispered. "All I can see are stars. There must be some wires down. Someone will fix them. Go back to bed."

Kelly didn't move. "I had a bad dream," she said.

Mom pulled Kelly close. "What about?"

"Mrs. Glocken was a sea monster."

Mom chuckled. "That's funny."

"No, it isn't. She was mean and scary-looking."

Mom rubbed Kelly's back. "Are you still worried about the programs?"

"A little."

"Are you upset about not having a special part in the concert?"

"Kind of."

"What else?"

Kelly sighed. "Oh, nothing. Just that there's nothing special about me."

Mom tapped Kelly on the tip of her nose. "You silly chickadee. You are special. Extra-special."

"You're just saying that because you're my mom."

Mom got out of bed and put on her robe. She took Kelly's hand. "Come on. Give me your flashlight. I want to show you something."

"Where are we going?"

"Shh. You'll see."

Mom led Kelly down the stairs. The flashlight made eerie yellow streaks on the walls. Kelly held onto Mom.

Mom unlocked the back door and led Kelly into the yard. She turned off the flashlight. "Look."

The earth was pure dark. The yard, the houses, the streets. But the sky shimmered with light. It looked like a box of silver glitter had spilled into the sky.

"I've never seen so many stars!" said Kelly. "Where were they before?"

Mom wrapped her robe around Kelly. "Those stars were there all the time, honey. Some stars are so far away, we can't see them until it gets really dark. There are millions of other stars that we still can't see. They're hiding in the heavens somewhere. Like you."

Kelly hugged Mom and smiled to herself. It was funny to think of a star hiding. Maybe that's just what she was.

9

"Turn that blasted thing down!" Dad yelled to Joe.

Joe's radio played loud music in the kitchen Friday morning. It was about the only thing working in the house.

The radio had batteries. Some of the clocks, like Kelly's, had batteries, too. Almost everything else — lights, refrigerator, stove — needed electricity. But there was no electricity.

"But, Dad," said Joe. "I'm waiting for the news. I bet there's no school today."

"Don't count on it," said Dad. "Now where is that instant coffee?" He was kneeling in the canned goods closet.

Kelly went over. "Up here, Daddy." She handed him the coffee jar. "I cleaned out the closet last week."

She flashed him a toothy grin that always made him smile. Not today. All Dad said was "Thanks." Boy, was he in a bad mood. Just because a bunch of wires didn't work.

Kelly was in a good mood. She was still feeling the magic of last night's starry sky.

Dad turned on the water. He spooned instant coffee into his mug and added hot water.

"Yuck," said Mom. "That looks horrible."

"Yuck!" said Scooter, laughing. "Yuck, yuck!"

Kelly smiled. "Mommy used your word, didn't she? Want me to feed you your cereal?"

Scooter pushed the bowl away. "No! Yuck, yuck, yuck!"

Mom sighed. "I couldn't warm up the milk for his oatmeal."

Kelly showed Scooter a banana. "Want this?"

Scooter bounced up and down in his high chair. "Na-na," he said, reaching for it.

Kelly peeled and mashed it on a plate with a fork.

"Good idea, honey," said Mom.

"Shh!" said Joe. "It's the local news." He had his ear next to the radio. He listened for a minute. "A couple other towns have no power, too. Something about the main transformer being down." He listened again.

"I don't believe it!" Joe flicked off the radio like he was killing a fly. "The schools have power. Now I'll get a zero in English today."

"Didn't you do your homework?" asked Dad.

"Sure," said Joe. "I did it on the computer. But I was going to print it out this morning. I have to turn in two copies. I'll never have time to write them both out."

Mom sighed. "You can at least get one done, can't you? That would be better than nothing."

Joe shrugged. "I guess so." He tore paper from his notebook and began writing.

Kelly jumped up. "I have some old carbon paper. You can make a second copy with it."

She ran up the steps two at a time.

Mom called to Kelly. "Make sure Trish is up."

Trish was still asleep. "Wake up," said Kelly. "Rise and shine!"

Trish rolled over and blinked. "Okay, okay."

Kelly looked in her desk. The carbon paper was in her art box, right where she knew it would be. She ran back down the stairs, holding up the carbon paper as if it were an A+ test. It was fun helping everyone.

"Thanks," said Joe.

45

Kelly smiled. "You're very welcome."

Julie was standing in the middle of the kitchen, frowning. She had clothes on each arm.

"Look at these outfits, Mom. One's wet and the other one's wrinkled. And I can't use the dryer or the iron."

"For goodness sakes, Julie," said Dad. "Wear something else."

"Oh, Dad," moaned Julie. "You don't understand."

"I have a great idea, Julie," said Kelly. "We'll light the outside grill and put some flat rocks in the fire. Then you can iron with the rocks! That's how people used to iron!"

Julie rolled her eyes. "Oh, Kelly. That's ridiculous! I'll just have to wear something ugly today." She stomped out of the kitchen.

Kelly folded her arms. "Gee. I was only trying to help."

Mom lifted Kelly's chin. "I know, honey. You've been such a great helper this morning. And your grill idea made me think of something. We can cook out tonight if the power's still off."

"Terrific!" said Kelly.

Trish padded into the kitchen in her pajamas.

"Good morning, sleepyhead," said Mom.

"Guess what!" said Trish. "None of the lights work!"

Mom and Dad laughed.

"We know all about it," said Joe.

"Wait till you hear this, Trish," said Kelly. "We're going to have a cookout tonight. And it's not even summer yet!"

"Yippee!" said Trish.

Kelly grinned. She was bursting with ideas today. She was bound to come up with an idea to fix the wrinkly programs.

10

Kelly and Trish made the bus just in time.

On the bus, Kelly unzipped her backpack, got out a big yellow envelope, and peeked inside. There was a stack of computer papers.

"What's that?" asked Trish.

"The stuff Bree did on the computer yesterday."

Kelly took the papers out.

There was a banner, a computer picture, and a sign that read: BREE'S ROOM. KEEP OUT. Then there was a poem.

"What's it say?" asked Trish.

Kelly read it out loud.

"The flowers miss Dad.
The pansies look sad.
The tulips bend down.
They're turning to brown.
The violets look blue.
I miss Daddy, too."

"Where's her dad?" asked Trish.

"In Florida."

Kelly was glad Trish didn't ask more. She didn't feel like explaining about Bree's parents being divorced.

She thought about what it would be like to have her parents divorced. It would be very sad. She didn't even like thinking about it. But something else was bothering her. She wasn't sure what it was.

"Hi, Kelly." Liza's voice startled her. Liza had gotten on the bus while Kelly was daydreaming.

"Whose poem?" asked Liza, as she squeezed in next to Kelly.

"Bree's. She wrote it at my house yesterday."

Liza read it. "Wow! That's really good — even if it is sad. I didn't know Bree could write poems. Boy, I wish I could do that."

"Me, too," said Kelly.

That was the thing that was bothering her.

That big old stupid "J" word. Jealous. Again. All because Bree could do something special. Bree would probably be a famous poet some day.

Sure. Kelly had been a terrific helper at home today. Big deal. Nobody really noticed except Mom. Moms were supposed to notice. That was their job.

"So, did you and Bree have fun yesterday?" asked Liza.

"Well, sort of," said Kelly, as she put the papers back in the envelope.

"I had scads of fun at Anna Mae's," said Liza. "There are all kinds of neat things to do at her house. And the tandem was best of all. Anna Mae's pretty nice when you get to know her."

"Great," said Kelly. She tried to make her voice sound like she meant it.

At school, the lights were on like Joe had said. But midway through the pledge of allegiance, the lights flickered twice. Mrs. Glocken was leading the pledge on the school loudspeaker. Her voice was cut into bits, like an astronaut reporting from outer space.

Kelly laughed. So did everyone.

Mrs. Hall frowned. She put her finger to her lips.

"We will now sing 'The Star-Spangled Banner.' " Mrs. Glocken's voice was loud and clear now.

Kelly rolled her eyes. She preferred "My Country 'Tis of Thee." Everyone could sing it better.

There was a pause. Kelly could picture Mrs. Glocken taking a big breath. Then her words came bursting out over the loudspeaker. "Oh, say, can you see?"

Suddenly the lights went out completely.

"Oh, say, I can't see!" Broderick sang loudly.

The kids broke into fits of giggles.

Kelly heard screams coming from the bathroom next door.

"Mrs. Hall," she called out, "may I go see what's wrong?"

"Go ahead. Quiet down now, everyone."

Kelly dashed out. She heard the first-grade class across the hall still singing. Mrs. Glocken, too. She was singing from the office way down the hall. "Whose broad stripes and bright stars . . ."

Kelly opened the bathroom door and looked in.

The bathroom was as dark as the hallway. Only a dim light came through the bumpy gray window.

"It's okay," called Kelly, from the doorway. "The lights are out everywhere."

51

"Wait for me!" said one voice.

"Me, too!" said another voice.

There was a double flush. Two scared-looking first graders ran toward the open door.

Out in the hall, Kelly looked hard at the bigger girl. "I know you! One time, you came over to my house to play with my sister Trish."

The girl shrugged. "I don't remember you. You're not Julie, are you?"

"No, I'm Kelly."

But the girl didn't hear her. She and her friend skipped back to their classroom.

All alone, Kelly stood frowning. "Yup," she said to herself. "I'm Kelly. Plain old ordinary Kelly."

11

The lights were still off at lunchtime.

Liza, Anna Mae, and Bree chattered between chews. Kelly ate in silence. She took a sip of orange drink. It tasted warm.

"I wish they were selling ice cream today," said Liza. "I don't care if it's melted. The Dixie cups probably taste like milkshakes."

Anna Mae laughed. She stirred her bowl of chili. "Good thing they have gas stoves in the kitchen," she said, "or the chili would be as cold as the ice cream."

"You mean chilly," said Bree. "It would be chilly chili!"

The girls laughed. Even Kelly.

"You're so funny, Bree," said Liza. "You write good poems, too."

"How do you know?" asked Bree.

"Kelly showed me the poem you wrote at her house."

Kelly swallowed the cookie she was chewing. "Oh, yeah, Bree. Joe gave me the papers you did yesterday. They're still in my backpack."

"Gosh. That was nice of him," said Bree. "Your whole family's nice."

"Thanks," said Kelly.

Bree turned to Liza and Anna Mae. "You should see Kelly's baby brother. He is the cutest thing. And her sister Trish is a model. Then the twins . . ."

"I know," Liza cut in. "I've been there hundreds of times."

Kelly looked at Liza in surprise. Liza sounded like the jealous one now. She didn't want Liza to be upset, but it was nice knowing that her best friend still cared.

Kelly got up to throw her trash away. Two teachers were chatting near the trash cans. They were talking about school letting out early. Kelly threw her trash away one piece at a time.

"The buses are supposed to be here right after the next lunch period," said one of the teachers.

"Unless the power comes on," said the other.

Kelly hot-footed back to the table.

"We're getting out early!" she announced to the girls.

"We know already," said Anna Mae. "Broderick told us while you were gone. Everyone knows."

"What am I going to do?" said Bree. "No one's home at my house. Mom's working. And Grandma doesn't come over until three o'clock. Can I go home with you again, Kelly? Your house is so much fun."

But before Kelly could answer, the lights went on again.

A chorus of kids yelled, "Boo!"

As if in reply, the bell rang. Everyone lined up.

Mrs. Glocken stood by the lunchroom door. She looked weird. Her hair was straight as straw. Maybe Mrs. Glocken's house had no electricity this morning, too. Maybe she couldn't use her curling iron.

"Listen now, all you second graders," said Mrs. Glocken in a regular voice. "I couldn't use the Xerox machine to make copies of the robin song. But I'll try this afternoon. Your teachers will pass them out before you go home today."

She let out a huge sigh. "Please, boys and girls, learn the words of the robin song. We don't want the singers on the record doing all the singing at the concert, do we?"

The kids snickered.

Mrs. Glocken pressed her lips into a puckered smile. "Now then," she sang. "I need all my second-grade stars."

Anna Mae, Mike, and Liza stepped out of line. So did some children in the other second-grade class.

Kelly shut her eyes. Why did Mrs. Glocken have to use the word "stars"?

"Where's Timmy?" asked Mrs. Glocken.

"Absent," said Anna Mae.

"I'll take his place," said Broderick.

"That's quite all right," said Mrs. Glocken. "I'm sure Timmy will be back in school by Monday."

Mrs. Glocken turned to Kelly. "How are the programs taking shape?"

Kelly wanted to shrink into her shoes. She looked at Bree, who was giggling behind her hands. Then it hit her. Taking shape.

"Fine," said Kelly, trying not to giggle herself. If only Mrs. Glocken knew what shape the programs were really in.

12

The power stayed on at school, but something was wrong with the copy machine. No one got copies of the robin song. Kelly didn't care. She already knew the words.

On the bus ride home, she wondered if the electricity was back on at her house. She hoped not.

Hoping didn't help. The power was on.

"Can we still cook out tonight?" she asked.

"Maybe," said Mom.

But long before dinner, it started to drizzle. Mom's "maybe" fizzled and turned into a "no."

"Some other time," said Mom.

By Saturday morning, the rain had stopped,

but the sky was still gray. It matched Kelly's mood.

She sat by a mountain of socks on the living-room rug. Matching everyone's socks was her Saturday job.

Sometimes Trish helped, but she was at a modeling job. Mom had taken her and Scooter into town right after breakfast.

Dad was gone, too. He had taken Julie to a baseball game.

Kelly was alone in the house with Joe, who was supposed to be ironing. But the iron stood still on the board.

Joe was in the kitchen, fooling around with the computer while he talked on the phone. Kelly could hear laughing and snorting above the computer beeps.

Kelly stared at the socks. Only the dark ones were left. The colored ones had been easy to match. They stood out as bright as traffic lights.

She picked up a dark blue sock and dug around in the pile, looking for its mate. She found one the same shade, but when she put the two together, they looked different. One was longer. The other felt smoother.

Kelly sighed. She hated matching socks. And when she was done with socks, she had the programs to do.

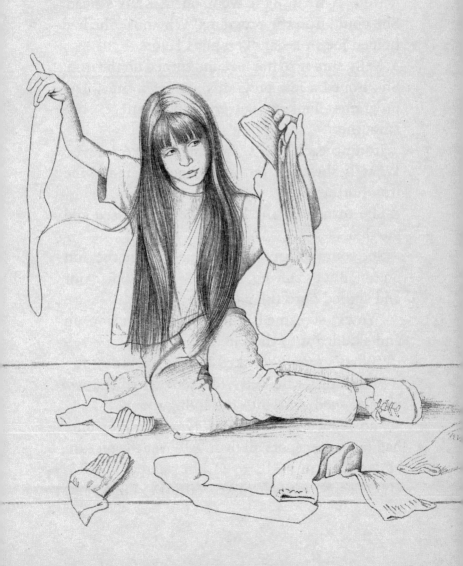

The programs were flatter from being under Mom's cookbooks. But they were as wrinkly as the clothes in the basket. The clothes Joe was supposed to iron.

Iron. A little light went on in Kelly's head. She could iron the programs! Why not? She had helped Joe iron handkerchiefs before.

Kelly sprang to her feet and turned on the iron. She ironed a few programs, one at a time. The programs looked better. Not perfect, but smoother.

Ironing each one was going to take forever. What if she tried ten at a time and made the iron hotter?

She turned up the heat. The iron hissed and gurgled.

She counted out ten programs and laid the iron on top. But as she did, boiling water bubbled out and spilled onto the papers.

"Yow!" screamed Kelly. She set the iron up and skidded into the kitchen.

"What's wrong?" asked Joe.

"Nothing," said Kelly. She took two dish towels and sped back into the living room.

She sopped up the water. Now the programs had tan water spots all over. All over the picture of a tandem. All over the names: MRS. GLOCKEN, ANNA MAE, TIMMY, LIZA, and all the other lucky second graders who had special parts.

So what? It was just ten programs. Programs that didn't have her name on them anyway. She could throw them away.

But what if Mrs. Glocken counted each one? What if she noticed that ten were missing? Kelly would have to hide them in the middle when they were dry.

But first she'd have to iron all the rest. And fold them. Not in half. That would have been easy. In thirds, like the sample.

Then she had to do the stupid socks.

Kelly felt like crying. She was sick of socks and Mrs. Glocken and programs.

13

"A frog went a-courtin', he did ride, uh huh," sang Kelly.

She sat on the rug in a circle of socks, pretending the socks were frogs. The sock frogs hopped around the circle until they found their mates. It was fun matching socks this way.

Outside the sun had burned away the gray. Kelly had decided to hurry with her chores so she could go outside.

She was almost finished with the socks and programs.

The programs were ironed but not folded yet. She hoped Mrs. Glocken wouldn't notice that they were not exactly flat and ten were freckled with spots.

"A frog went a-courtin', he did ride, uh huh," someone sang through the window screen.

Kelly looked up in surprise. "Liza!"

"Hi, Kelly. Whatcha doing? Singing to your socks?"

Kelly blushed. "No, just singing while I work." She pushed the socks back into a big pile and covered the programs with a shirt from the clothes basket.

Inside, Liza grabbed Kelly's arm. "I need your help."

"What's wrong?"

"Oh, Kelly, I'm so worried about the concert. I don't know all the words to the robin song yet. Will you teach me?"

Kelly smiled. "Sure." It was nice to be needed. Especially by Liza.

"That's funny," said Liza. She was looking at the shirt on top of the programs. "That looks just like our school T-shirts that we all got from the PTA. But that one's enormous!"

"It's Dad's," said Kelly. "He and Mom bought shirts for themselves when we got our free ones."

"I knew it wasn't yours," said Liza. "It would be as long as a dress on you. Look." She picked

up the blue shirt with the words FEATHER-STONE SCHOOL and held it up to Kelly.

A few programs slid to the floor. "Oops," said Liza. "Ew! They look funny. What happened to them?"

Kelly put the programs back. She sighed. "There's a lot to tell."

"So tell me."

"Well, it all started when I was pretending to be a flamingo."

Liza giggled. "A flamingo?"

Kelly told the whole story. It didn't seem so terrible now that she had told Liza.

"What do you think Mrs. Glocken will say?" asked Liza.

"I don't know. If she doesn't see these spotted programs first, maybe she won't notice."

"Who won't notice?" said Joe, as he walked into the living room. "What did you do now, Kelly?"

"Nothing at all. Come on, Liza, let's go out-side."

Kelly wanted to push Mrs. Glocken out of her mind. Deep down, she knew Mrs. Glocken would notice that something was very wrong with the programs.

The girls sat on the swings and sang the robin song twice together.

"You're still messing up some of the words," said Kelly. She wanted to say, "I should be the robin in the concert. I know all the words." Instead, she said, "Maybe I should sing it alone so you can hear the words better."

"Good idea," said Liza. "Go up on the deck. It can be the stage. I'll be the audience."

"Okay," said Kelly. "But I'll have to skip the whistling part." She scrambled up the steps to the deck. This was going to be fun.

She looked down. Liza had pulled a lawn chair over.

Kelly closed her eyes for a moment and pretended she was a star on the stage at Featherstone School. She pretended that Liza was sitting with hundreds of people.

She took a deep breath and started to sing. She sang the whole, long song as loud and clear as she could.

Liza clapped. "Hey, Kelly, that was terrific!"

The lady from next door called from her yard. "What pretty singing, honey."

"It's Fanny of the Opera again," Joe shouted through the window. "Bravo, Fanny, bravo."

Joe's teasing didn't bother Kelly. She knew she had sung well. She smiled and danced down the steps of the deck.

"Did you hear the words all right?" she asked Liza.

"Sure. I just don't remember them yet. I wish Mrs. Glocken had made copies yesterday."

"I could write down the words," said Kelly, "but I won't be able to spell them all."

"Joe can help, can't he?"

"I guess so," said Kelly. Then she clapped her hands together. "I know. He can put it on the computer and print out enough copies for everyone! Let's go ask him."

Kelly and Liza scampered into the kitchen. Kelly made a deal with Joe. She'd iron the handkerchiefs if he typed out the robin song on the computer.

"I can't believe your teacher is having second graders sing this long, ridiculous song," said Joe, as he started on the last line.

Suddenly the screen went blank. The desk light went out. The refrigerator got quiet.

"Not again!" said Joe. "The power's off."

In a blink, it was on again.

"Thank goodness," said Liza.

"I hate to tell you, girls," said Joe, "but your song is gone. Wiped out. Kaput."

"What do you mean?" asked Kelly.

"I didn't save it on the disk before the power

went out. Sorry. But I'm not starting over. I have ironing to do. Unless you want to do the whole basket, Kelly."

"No way! Can't you type the words later? Like tomorrow?"

"Maybe," said Joe. "We'll see."

"Rats!" said Kelly. She hated "maybe's" and "we'll see's." Especially from Joe. It was bad enough when Mom and Dad said them.

Liza smiled. "It's okay, Kelly. Come on. I'll help you fold the programs."

Kelly smiled at Liza. "Thanks."

Liza was a true friend. She wanted to hug her. At least give her something. Like the words of the robin song. Tomorrow, she would talk Joe into typing them.

14

Monday morning, on the bus ride to school, Kelly handed Liza an envelope. There were bird stickers all over it.

"Oo! How pretty! What's inside?"

"Open it," said Kelly.

Liza did.

"Wow! You wrote down all the words of the robin song! Thanks, Kelly."

"We couldn't use the computer," said Kelly. "Julie needed it all yesterday for a big report."

Liza spread the paper on her lap. "It must have taken you ages to write this."

Kelly nodded. "It took forever."

She stretched out her right hand. "Look. I

have a bump on my finger from squeezing the pencil."

"Aw, Kelly, that was so nice."

"Thanks." Kelly smiled.

Monday morning was starting out just fine. When she got to school, she was going to go see Mrs. Glocken. First thing. She was going to hand her the bag of programs, sealed tight with tape.

Then, before Mrs. Glocken would have time to open it, Kelly would talk. She knew exactly what she would say. She hoped Mrs. Glocken acted as happy as Liza had.

As soon as Kelly hung up her jacket, she asked Mrs. Hall if she could deliver the programs.

"Sure, honey."

Kelly hurried down the hallway. Her heart pounded. Timmy wasn't in school again. Now she had something else to say to Mrs. Glocken. It was going to be a real speech.

As she neared the supply room, she heard humming. She peeked in the open doorway.

Mrs. Glocken was sitting at her desk, painting her nails. Kelly wondered if she should knock. Or maybe she should leave the programs on the floor by the door. She could talk to Mrs. Glocken later. She sighed.

"Who's out there?" Mrs. Glocken sang out.

Kelly swallowed hard and stepped inside the supply room.

"Why, good morning, Kelly," said Mrs. Glocken. She screwed on the nail-polish lid.

Kelly laid the bag on the desk. "Here are the programs. I hope they're okay."

She took a deep breath. "My brother can type the robin song on his computer today. We'll make copies to give out to everyone. Did you know that Timmy is absent again? I can take his place. I have a green jumpsuit. I can . . ."

"Whoa, Kelly. Hold your horses," said Mrs. Glocken. "First of all, I've already made copies of the robin song. I'll be handing them out today."

Kelly frowned. She rubbed the bump on her finger. Liza won't need mine now, she thought.

Mrs. Glocken smiled. "Thank you very much, anyway. As far as Timmy goes, his mother says he'll be here tomorrow. He's a little worried about being the frog, so we'll need to cheer him on. He's never had a chance to do something special."

Kelly bit her lip. She wanted to say, "What about me?"

Mrs. Glocken got up from her desk, blowing on her shiny red nails.

"Now then. I better skedaddle to the office for the pledge of allegiance."

She swished past Kelly. "Thank you for doing the programs, dear. I'm sure they're just perfect."

Perfect. The word burned in Kelly's ears.

15

"Broderick Hess!" Mrs. Glocken hissed. "Lock your lips until it's time to sing. That goes for everyone."

Broderick pulled out his lips and pretended to lock them.

Mrs. Glocken frowned. She turned around and began walking again. The two second-grade classes followed her in a long snake of a line.

They were heading for the gym. Kelly never wanted to get there. She knew why Mrs. Glocken was in a bad mood. She must have seen the programs.

When Kelly passed the supply room, she looked in. Sure enough, the programs were not on Mrs. Glocken's desk anymore.

In the gym, the kids sat on the floor.

Kelly looked up at the stage. Long steps stretched across like bleachers. She remembered them from last year. They were called risers.

Mrs. Glocken folded her arms and scowled. "Boys and girls, I have two announcements."

There was no music in Mrs. Glocken's voice. Kelly wished she could squeeze herself into a ball and quietly roll away.

"Number one." Mrs. Glocken held up one spiky finger. Kelly sucked in her breath. Any second, that finger would point to her.

"Just a little while ago," said Mrs. Glocken, "I found out that we can't have our concert on Friday."

As if on cue, the kids murmured, "Aww!"

Kelly's stomach jumped. Were the programs bad enough to cancel the whole concert?

"Instead of Friday, it will be on Wednesday. This Wednesday. The day after tomorrow."

Mrs. Glocken heaved a great sigh. "And I don't think we are ready," she added in a whisper.

"Number two."

Here it comes, thought Kelly.

"You are to wear your blue school T-shirts for the concert. Wear them with long pants. Girls, you may wear skirts, if you prefer."

"Me, too?" asked Anna Mae.

"No," said Mrs. Glocken. "You'll still be dressed for your part as Daisy. The same goes for everyone with special parts."

"My mom just bought me a dress for the concert," said Bree.

Mrs. Glocken shook her head. "I'm sorry. But the principal wants everyone dressed alike."

Mrs. Glocken sounded as disappointed as Bree. Disappointed about the T-shirts and the new concert day. And the programs. At least she hadn't said anything in front of everyone. Not yet.

"Rats!" Bree whispered. "I wanted to wear my new dress."

Kelly knew how Bree felt. She had planned to wear a dress that had been Julie's. She didn't usually like hand-me-downs, but this dress was beautiful. It sparkled with sequins and bright painted flowers.

Now Kelly would look like everyone else. Only the stars would stand out, just like colored socks in a pile of dark ones.

"Now then," said Mrs. Glocken. "Children with special parts, stand over here. The rest of you, line up along the wall by size. Tall children down to the shortest ones."

Mrs. Glocken moved everyone around. Her

fingers snapped and pointed. Her mouth never smiled. Her voice never sang. Kelly tried to dodge Mrs. Glocken's frowny eyes.

The stars got up onstage and stood on one side. The tall kids climbed onto the highest riser in back. The regular-size kids filed onto the next riser down.

Kelly walked with the shortest group onto the third riser.

"Look at the children beside you," said Mrs. Glocken, "and remember where you're standing."

Kelly was between two boys from the other second-grade room. She didn't know the one on her right. The one on her left had been in her kindergarten class. She didn't remember his name. But she would have no trouble remembering where she was standing. She was smack dab in the middle of the riser.

Everyone would be able to see her even when the first graders stood on the bottom three risers.

Mrs. Glocken stood on the gym floor, hands on her hips. Kelly saw her eyes sweep across the rows of kids, stacked like layers on a wedding cake.

In her center spot, Kelly felt as eye-catching as a flower made from frosting. She waited for Mrs. Glocken to scold her about the programs.

But Mrs. Glocken said nothing. She bent down and plugged in the record player. Then she rooted around in a big cardboard box. "Flying fiddlesticks!" she said.

The kids snickered.

That's it, thought Kelly. Mrs. Glocken just got a good look at the programs.

"Bree," said Mrs. Glocken, "I must have left the concert record in the supply room. Please go and see if it's on the shelf behind my desk. Make it snappy."

Bree scampered down the stage steps and out the gym door.

Mrs. Glocken dug around in the box again.

Kelly couldn't stand it any longer. She stepped off the risers and went to the edge of the stage.

"Excuse me," she whispered to the back of Mrs. Glocken's head.

Mrs. Glocken half turned, her hands still in the box.

"What is it?"

Kelly gulped. "I'm so sorry about the programs. They got wet by mistake. And then when I ironed them . . ."

"The programs looked fine to me," said Mrs. Glocken. "The only problem is that the date on them is wrong now. But we can't help that, can we?"

Bree was back. She handed over the record.

Mrs. Glocken waved Kelly away. "Back to your place. It's time to sing."

Kelly went back to her spot, blinking back tears. She should be happy. Mrs. Glocken hadn't even noticed that something was wrong with the programs. But that was the problem. Mrs. Glocken never seemed to notice anything about her.

16

"And now, here is the star of Featherstone School — Miss Kelly McKay!" Julie pushed open the swinging door and waved Kelly into the kitchen where everyone was having breakfast.

Kelly danced into the room. It was Wednesday morning, the day of the Spring Concert. She was dressed in the same blue T-shirt that all the kids would be wearing.

But Kelly looked different. She wore Dad's big T-shirt. Just like Liza had said, it was as long as a dress.

Julie had lent Kelly her neon yellow tights and belt to match the words FEATHERSTONE SCHOOL. She had brushed Kelly's hair, clipped

a barrette of colored feathers on the side, and tied a string of feathers around her neck.

"K-K!" Scooter called out.

"Wow-ee, Kelly," said Trish, "I wish I looked like you."

"That's why you wanted my T-shirt," said Dad. "It looks cute on you."

Joe clapped. "Wooo, Fanny!"

"WOOO!" cried Scooter.

"Give me my sunglasses," said Joe. "You're way too bright!"

"Stop it, Joe," said Julie. "She looks nice. Don't you think, Mom?"

Mom was staring at Kelly, her head tilted to the side.

"What's the matter, Mom?" asked Kelly.

"Nothing, sweetie. I'm just not used to seeing you dressed that way. I'm not sure I like the feathers."

"They go with the 'F' in Featherstone," said Kelly. "See how the 'F' looks like a feather?"

"Yes," said Mom. "But I want you to know you're just as pretty without all the frills."

Kelly smiled. "Thanks, Mom. But today I want to look special onstage."

"What about me?" said Trish. "I want some feathers to go with my T-shirt, too."

"No," said Kelly. "I don't want you copying me."

"I don't have any more feathers anyway," said Julie. "I'll let you wear them another day, Trish."

"Phooey." Trish stuck out her lip. "I want to be as pretty as Kelly."

"Oh, Trish, you're always pretty," said Kelly. "For once, I want to be the one that's noticed."

Kelly got what she wanted. As soon as she stepped on the bus, Mr. Jackson whistled. "Don't you look spiffy!" he said.

When Liza got on the bus, her mouth dropped open. "You're a knockout. Wait till everyone sees you."

In class, the girls made a circle around her. They "oohed" and "aahed" as if she were a rare tropical bird.

"What a great idea," said Bree.

"What's so great about it?" said Anna Mae. "Haven't you ever seen someone wear an over-sized T-shirt before?" She sounded grumpy.

Anna Mae was probably mad that no one was saying anything about her outfit. She was wearing a fancy dress and a big hair bow for her part as Daisy.

Mrs. Hall flicked the lights. "All right. Settle

down and get in your seats. You all look so nice for the concert today." She winked at Kelly. "Some of you really went all out."

Kelly sat at her desk, but she felt as if she could float out of her seat any minute. All the nice words sailed around in her head.

"Try to stay as neat as you can," said Mrs. Hall, "since the concert isn't until the end of the day."

Kelly scratched her neck. It itched from the feathers.

Her tights felt funny. They were too long. She pulled them up where they had slipped into wrinkles by her feet. It was going to be hard waiting all day.

In the middle of math, the school nurse walked into class.

"I need to get everyone's weight and height," she told Mrs. Hall. "It will only take a few minutes."

Everyone got in line. The nurse led the class to her tiny office. The first two children went in. Kelly stood with the rest against the hallway wall, waiting for her turn.

She heard Broderick talking like a parrot way behind her. "Pretty parrot, pretty parrot," he said loudly. "Kelly wanta cracker? Kelly wanta cracker?"

The boys exploded with laughter. Even some of the girls laughed.

"Don't pay any attention to them," Liza told Kelly.

But it was hard not to. The nurse came out to shush them, but the teasing and giggling just got softer.

A fifth-grade class walked by. Kelly felt like they were all staring at her. Two girls whispered to each other and snickered.

Finally it was Kelly's turn to see the nurse. She was glad to get out of the hallway.

The nurse gave her a surprised look. "My word, Kelly. You're as pretty as a peacock today."

"Thanks," said Kelly. But she wasn't sure she wanted to look like a peacock. Certainly not a parrot.

Instead of looking like a star, maybe she looked ridiculous. When the nurse was done checking her, she dashed into the bathroom.

She stared in the mirror. In her head, she heard, "Way too bright . . . Kelly wanta cracker. . . . Pretty as a peacock."

Kelly whipped off the feathers. She fixed her tights, fluffed her hair, and scooted back to class. She would have to be a star without feathers.

17

Kelly stood in her center spot onstage, waiting for the Spring Concert to begin. The air was thick with whispers and scuffing feet.

"Let's get the show on the road," she heard Bree mutter behind her.

She stared at the purple curtain, closed tight. Mom and Scooter sat somewhere on the other side. She hoped they had gotten good seats. But even if they hadn't, they'd see her right away.

The first graders filed onto the stage and filled up the bottom three risers.

Kelly let out a burst of breath like a pin-popped balloon. "I don't believe it," she said to herself.

The heads of the first graders were higher than

she thought they'd be. She could barely see over a frizzy-haired boy.

Some star she'd be now. Her fancy feathers were gone. Her curls had sagged. Her bright tights and belt were hidden.

She was plain old ordinary Kelly again. No one special. Just another face in a blur of blue T-shirts.

Mrs. Glocken poked her head through the curtains.

"Shh! It's time. Now remember — when the curtains open, sing along with the piano while the kindergarten comes up onstage."

The whispering and scuffing stopped. The stage was silent.

Kelly's stomach flip-flopped. How silly. She wasn't doing anything special. Not like the stars. They were going to be right out front.

They had a reason to be jittery. And they looked it. Timmy chewed on his nails. Liza kept licking her lips. Mike rocked from side to side. Even Anna Mae looked nervous. The stars from the other second grade didn't look any better.

The curtains opened. Mrs. Glocken thundered out the notes on the piano.

"Sing, sing a song," everyone sang, as the kindergarten kids climbed up the steps to line up onstage.

Kelly spotted Trish. She gave a small wave, but Trish didn't see her.

She looked out at the audience. The gym was filled with third, fourth, and fifth graders, and parents, brothers, and sisters. Mom and Scooter were easy to find. They sat in the row right behind the empty seats for the kindergarten kids.

Mom had Scooter on her lap. She pointed to the stage. Kelly could imagine Mom saying, "There's Kelly. See? Right in the middle. Right behind that boy."

But Kelly could tell Scooter didn't see her. The only sister he saw was Trish.

The kindergarten children sang their two songs and left the stage. The audience clapped.

Kelly watched Trish sit down right near Mom and Scooter.

Mrs. Glocken played the piano as the first graders sang three songs by themselves. Then she got up and turned on the record player. It was time for the second graders. Kelly wished the first graders would leave, but they stayed put.

Mrs. Glocken set the needle on the record and went to stand on a small wooden box on the gym floor. She faced the stage, flushed and smiling, her hands out like a traffic cop.

The music started. Mrs. Glocken's arms

flapped in time with the beat. Her mouth moved with the words.

Two second-grade girls wearing pink dresses and paper pig snouts skipped in front of the risers. Giggles rippled through the audience.

The girls hooked arms, as they sang and spun around. A pig snout flew off one girl's face. Both girls bent down to get it. The other snout came off. The giggling grew louder.

The girls' faces were pinker than their dresses. But they smiled and kept singing.

Kelly felt sorry for them. She wondered what she would have done. She probably would have run off the stage at the first giggle.

The next two songs went better. Three songs were left. Kelly's favorites.

"A frog went a-courtin', he did ride, uh huh," the record player blared, as the second graders sang.

Timmy stood in his Kermit the Frog sweatsuit on the side of the stage. He was supposed to be hopping and singing with the music. Anna Mae gave him a push. He didn't move. The song went on without Timmy.

Kelly heard Broderick say, "I knew he couldn't do it. I could have been a better frog."

Kelly turned around and glared at him. Broderick could have been a better frog. So could she.

But it didn't help saying that now.

"Come on, Timmy," Kelly said in her head.

Mrs. Glocken's eyes were begging Timmy to move. But Timmy stayed glued to one spot.

The song was almost over.

Kelly could hardly stand it. "Come on, Timmy," she said out loud. "You can do it."

Timmy looked up. With a sudden burst of pep, he hopped across the stage and back.

The song ended. Clapping filled the air. Timmy was red-faced, but smiling. Kelly closed her eyes and let out a long breath.

There was a clank and clatter of metal off-stage. Kelly looked. The tandem had fallen on its side. Anna Mae and Mike tried to set it back up.

The song was in full swing when they finally wheeled the two-seater out onstage. Anna Mae looked flustered, but she sang and swayed, like a born star. When the song ended, she blew a kiss to Mike. Mike made a face. Everyone laughed.

Kelly rolled her eyes. Anna Mae really knew how to ham it up. She didn't mind that people were laughing at her.

Kelly would have minded. Good thing she wasn't a star. She would have been as scared as Timmy.

She looked down at Liza, dressed like a robin

with a paper beak and wings. She was glad she wasn't in her shoes.

Liza walked to the middle of the stage and fluttered her wings. The robin song started.

Kelly stood tall and sang out the words she loved. She could hardly hear the voices around her. Mrs. Glocken had given out copies of the words, but it must not have helped much.

Suddenly, the lights went out and the record player stopped. A murmur of moans hummed in the dark gym. The singing fizzled.

Oh, no, thought Kelly. The electricity's gone again.

18

Two funny-looking lights came on in the corners of the gym. They cast an eerie glow on the sea of faces.

Kelly saw Mom, Scooter, and Trish watching the stage. She saw Mrs. Glocken, white-faced and wide-eyed, staring at Liza.

Poor Liza. She was standing all alone on the dark, quiet stage. She turned around and looked up at Kelly. Her eyes said, "Now what?"

Kelly shrugged. "Fly off the stage," she wanted to tell her. But Liza stayed rooted to her spot, like a plant instead of a bird.

Mrs. Glocken should tell someone to close the curtains. Kelly could see the ropes peeking out of the purple folds. She should pull them herself. She could sneak behind the backs of the tall first graders and jump down onto the stage.

But Kelly couldn't move. She felt like she had roots, too. Bree tapped her on the back. "Guess we'll have to wing it," she whispered.

Wing it. Bree was making a joke again. Or was she? Could they really sing without the record player?

Liza looked at Kelly again. This time, Liza mouthed a simple, single word. "Help!"

Kelly gave a small nod. "Okay," she said to herself. "I'll try."

Her heart thumped hard. She started to sing the words of the chorus. They were the easy words. Right away, all the second graders joined in.

Mrs. Glocken sang, too. Her arms flapped out the beat again.

Kelly started in on the hard words of the second verse. The voices around her faded. She pretended she was back on the deck at home, singing loud enough for the lady next door.

Some first graders turned around and stared at her. She could tell the boys beside her were staring, too. Little by little, more voices blended with Kelly's.

After the second verse, the singing got loud

for the chorus. Then soft again for the third verse.

Kelly belted out the words. It was fun singing in the dark, hidden behind the frizzy-haired boy.

She remembered Mom's words the night they looked at the star-filled sky. *Those stars were there all the time . . . hiding in the heavens somewhere. Like you.*

Near the end of the last verse, Kelly stopped singing. It was the whistling part. She couldn't help Liza now.

Liza fluttered her wings and whistled. Only a few kids joined in, but she was doing fine on her own. She whistled a walloping tune.

Liza tweeted her last note. Then Kelly led the singing of the chorus until the end of the song.

The audience was silent for a moment. Then a shrill, little voice cut through the quiet. "K-K, K-K!"

Scooter! Kelly almost laughed out loud. She looked. Scooter was bouncing on Mom's lap. "K-K," he called again.

A smatter of giggles turned into a roar of applause.

Mrs. Glocken had a smile as wide as a keyboard. She faced the audience and swept her arm toward the stage. The clapping grew louder.

The applause was as sweet as a song. Kelly

knew that some of it was meant for her.

Liza flashed her a smile.

"Way to go, Kelly," said Bree.

When the clapping died down, Mrs. Glocken went up onstage. She announced the names of the second-grade stars. They came out front and bowed. The clapping started again.

Mrs. Glocken held up her hand. "There's one more special second grader."

Kelly's knees suddenly felt like Jell-O. Was she the one?

Mrs. Glocken continued. "Her perfectly lovely voice led the singing when we needed her the most. Kelly McKay! Come on out wherever you are and take a bow!"

Fireworks flashed in Kelly's head. The applause was just for her now.

Somehow she used her Jell-O knees to climb down to the stage floor. Then plain old ordinary Kelly McKay smiled the smile of a star and bowed.

About the Author

Nancy Markham Alberts relives her own childhood through her writing. Her years as an elementary schoolteacher, and the antics of her school-age children and their friends, provide additional inspiration.

She grew up in southern New Jersey, but now lives near Pittsburgh, Pennsylvania, with her husband and their two children.

LITTLE 🍎 APPLE®

Here are some of our favorite Little Apples.

Once you take a bite out of a Little Apple book—you'll want to read more!

Books for Kids with BIG Appetites!

- ❏ NA45899-X **Amber Brown Is Not a Crayon**
  Paula Danziger $2.99
- ❏ NA42833-0 **Catwings** Ursula K. LeGuin $3.50
- ❏ NA42832-2 **Catwings Return** Ursula K. LeGuin $3.50
- ❏ NA41821-1 **Class Clown** Johanna Hurwitz $3.50
- ❏ NA42400-9 **Five True Horse Stories** Margaret Davidson $3.50
- ❏ NA42401-7 **Five True Dog Stories** Margaret Davidson $3.50
- ❏ NA43868-9 **The Haunting of Grade Three**
  Grace Maccarone $3.50
- ❏ NA40966-2 **Rent a Third Grader** B.B. Hiller $3.50
- ❏ NA41944-7 **The Return of the Third Grade Ghost Hunters**
  Grace Maccarone $2.99
- ❏ NA47463-4 **Second Grade Friends** Miriam Cohen $3.50
- ❏ NA45729-2 **Striped Ice Cream** Joan M. Lexau $3.50

Available wherever you buy books...or use the coupon below.

- -

SCHOLASTIC INC., P.O. Box 7502, 2931 East McCarty Street, Jefferson City, MO 65102

Please send me the books I have checked above. I am enclosing $ _____ (please add $2.00 to cover shipping and handling). Send check or money order—no cash or C.O.D.s please.

Name_____

Address_____

City_____State/Zip_____

Please allow four to six weeks for delivery. Offer good in the U.S.A. only. Sorry, mail orders are not available to residents of Canada. Prices subject to change.   LAP198